CLEAN ENOUGH

by Kevin Henkes

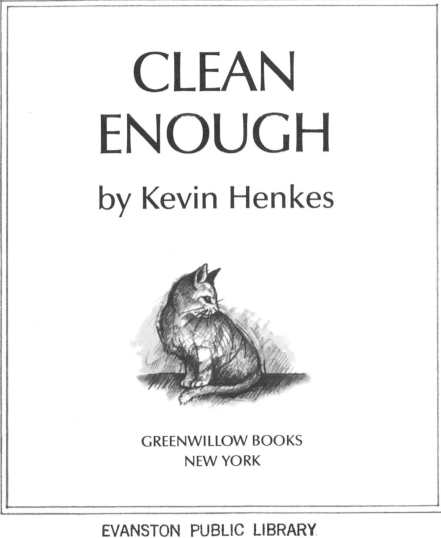

GREENWILLOW BOOKS
NEW YORK

Library of Congress
Cataloging in Publication Data
Henkes, Kevin.   Clean enough.
Summary: A little boy finds more to enjoy
in the bath than just washing himself.
[1.   Baths—Fiction]   I   Title.
PZ7.H389C!   [E]   81-6386
ISBN 0-688-00828-3   AACR2
ISBN 0-688-00829-1 (lib. bdg.)

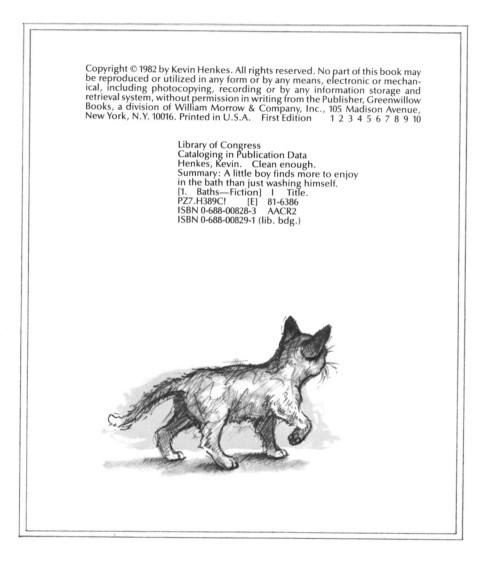

For Dad

remember?

When I take a bath,
I leave the door open just a little

and I keep my towel right next
to the tub in case I get soap
in my eyes.

Sometimes it's hard to get the water
to feel just right. Once my father
let me put a whole tray of ice cubes
in the water to cool it off.
It didn't work.

I try turning the handles the same
amount, but usually the water's still
too hot or too cold.

The water finally feels okay.
I just sit in it.

I think that I must be getting bigger
because the tub seems smaller
every time.

When I was real little and my father
gave me my bath, he would hold
a soaked washcloth over my stomach
and let the drips splash on me.

I try it.
It doesn't tickle like it used to.

I pretend the soap dish is a raft.
I lie in the tub and move under the water
to make waves. My raft sails,

until I sink it!

Once I took my father's shaving cream
and made foamy stripes
on my arms and legs.

Then I pretended that the soap
was a tiny cake and I frosted it.

Just when I was starting to write
my name on the water,
my mother made me get out.

Now she's calling me again.
She says to hurry up because
my little brother has to take a bath too.
I haven't even started to wash yet,
but I've been in the tub a very long time,

so I must be clean enough.